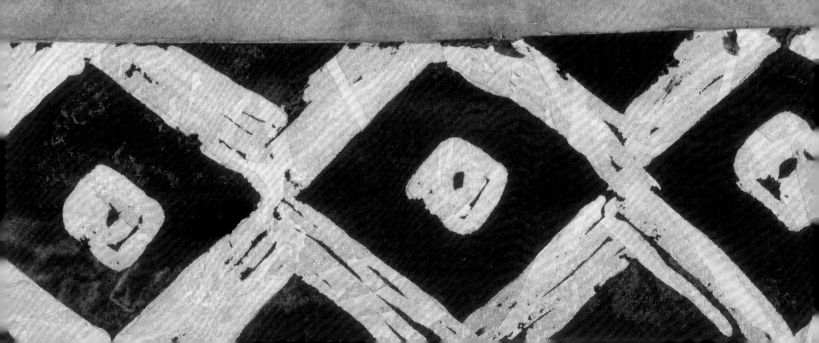

The
EVERLASTING
EMBRACE

GABRIELLE EMANUEL

illustrated by E. B. LEWIS

VIKING

An Imprint of Penguin Group (USA)

VIKING

Published by the Penguin Group

Penguin Group (USA) LLC

375 Hudson Street, New York, New York 10014

USA ❀ Canada ❀ UK ❀ Ireland ❀ Australia ❀ New Zealand ❀ India ❀ South Africa ❀ China

penguin.com

A Penguin Random House Company

First published in the United States of America by Viking, an imprint of Penguin Young Readers Group, 2014

Text copyright © 2014 by Gabrielle Emanuel

Illustrations copyright © 2014 by E. B. Lewis

LIBRARY OF CONGRESS CATALOGING-IN-PUBLICATION DATA

Emanuel, Gabrielle.

The everlasting embrace / by Gabrielle Emanuel ; illustrated by E. B. Lewis.

pages cm

Summary: A young child describes her experiences of life in Mali as she spends a day carried in a blanket on her mother's back.

ISBN 978-0-670-78474-5 (hardcover)

[1. Mother and child—Fiction. 2. Mali—Fiction.] I. Lewis, Earl B., illustrator. II. Title.

PZ7.E564Eve 2014

[E]—dc23

2014001447

Manufactured in China

1 3 5 7 9 10 8 6 4 2

Book design by Nancy Brennan

Set in Cooper Old Style

The Chi Wara, a mystical figure depicted on the facing page, is a common motif in Mali. It is believed that this
antelope-like creature taught the Bamana people of Mali how to farm. Female Chi Waras carry babies on their backs.
It is often said this relationship symbolizes how the earth sustains humans.

*To my parents and siblings, who have given me
a virtual embrace my whole life.* —G.E.

To Linda Kehm-Rich, my assistant, whom I adore. —E.B.L.

EACH AND EVERY MORNING, my mother and I greet the day the exact same way.

As the sun brightens the sky and bids the horizon good-bye, my mother leans over halfway and lays me on her back. Her expert hands tie a blanket snugly around me and then wrap it in a knot on her front.

We are bound together.

Rising up straight and tall, we beckon the day toward us.
I sit comfortably in my little cocoon. My mother says I am
bound close to her by a thread she has woven.
This day and every day, my mother spends with me. And I
spend it with my mother.

As the sun creeps higher and higher in the sky, I am lulled by my mother's rhythmic pounding of millet. Lifting the pestle high above our heads, we slam it into the mortar. Together, we grind the grain into a powder.

My mother tells me that I am sitting in a seat reserved just for me. I have a front row seat on the world, where I can watch everything that happens.

I count the donkeys that plod past us, the boats that paddle by us, and the motorcycles that zip down the path before us, as my mother carries the ground millet back to our house.

Cuddled to her back, I do not have to hold on to my mother,
and she does not have to hold on to me. We are simply one.

I peep around the folds of my mother's clothes to see what her hands are doing. Sometimes they are busy pulling buckets of water from the square well by our house.

But when my mother's hands are free, they become teasing rascals. Finding their way to my feet, her hands tickle me and make me squirm in my pouch.

My mother tells me that we dance through our days together, always in perfect step with one another.

She sets the rhythm, leading our dance. Right foot. Left foot. Tiptoe. Squat down. Bounce, bounce, bounce.

We float past fruit stands. We jump over streams during the rainy season. And we tiptoe around the branches that clutter the ground in the dry season.

When my eyes well up and leak tears, my mother does a special little step with her feet to soothe me to sleep.

When I wake from my midday nap, my eyes look to the horizon and watch the sun crescendo in its own dance across the sky. My mother whispers to me that we are fortunate, for we get to sit underneath our own personal umbrella.

Balanced atop my mother's head is a large bowl of sweet mangos. The smell drifts down and draws us onward with the unspoken promise that a treat awaits.

Brimming with summer's golden gift, the bowl sits above our heads. When the sun's gaze is the hottest, this umbrella of mangos provides welcome shade wherever we need it.

My mother and I share everything. We even share our play dates. Whenever my mother greets her friend, I peek around my mother's back and smile at my friend.

Walking slowly down the street, my mother and her friend chatter away. Sitting on their backs, my friend and I giggle as we try to hold hands.

Day after day we spend together. My mother tells me that I am growing bigger and bigger.

Soon, she says, I will grow too big to ride in my little cocoon. I will be too big to sit in my front row seat, watching the world.

We walk through the outdoor market
together. The booths overflow with colors and sounds.

My mother stops in front of a stall where stuffed animals dangle on strings.

Sifting through the baskets filled with teddy bears, my mother picks out a baby bear for me.

When we get home, my mother kneels to help me place the bear on my back. Tying a blanket around the bear and me, my mother whispers in my ear. She says it is my job to carry the baby bear and lead her through our days.

My mother tells me that I am her little butterfly that has emerged from my cocoon, ready to explore the world.

But my mother promises that I will never grow too big to dance with her. Soon, she says, I can lead our dances and find new rhythms.

Later, as we watch the moon's glow brighten the night sky, I tell my mother that we are lucky because our hug is neverending.

Most people hug for just a moment. They hug fleetingly
to say hello, good-bye, or thank you.

But parents and children share an everlasting embrace
that endures our whole lives.

A few of the many photographs
I took while living in Mali.

I ni sɛ!
Greetings!

MALI is a country nestled in the heart of West Africa. I moved there after graduating from college. Over the course of a year, I learned to navigate the brilliantly colorful marketplaces, appreciate the elegance of Mali's mud architecture and stone structures, and participate in the constant activity that defines life in the family compounds.

In the evenings after work and after a communal dinner, I would read stories to a little girl. As I read the words, I worried that there were no characters from her own culture. So I started making up and writing down new stories for the local children, stories that reflected their own country and culture.

This story grew out of the fact that Mali has one of the world's highest birthrates. Thus almost all of the women I met carried a young child bound to their back. I found myself imagining what it would be like to grow up experiencing the world from that child's perspective.

I hope this story captures the mother-child love that is both unique and universal.

Kambufo, k'an bɛn.
Good-bye, until we meet again.
—*Gabrielle*